Inch by Inch

by Leo Lionni

HarperCollinsPublishers

Inch by Inch
Copyright © 1960 by Leo Lionni
Manufactured in Hong Kong. All rights reserved.
Reprinted by arrangement with
Astor–Honor Publishing Inc.

Library of Congress Cataloging-in-Publication Data
Leo, Lionni.
    Inch by inch / by Leo Lionni.
        p.   cm.
    Summary: To keep from being eaten, an inchworm measures a
robin's tail, a flamingo's neck, a toucan's beak, a heron's legs,
and a nightingale's song.
    ISBN 0-688-13283-9
    [1. Worms—Fiction. 2. Birds—Fiction.]
I. Title.
PZ7.L6634Ip   1995   94-6483
[E]—dc20   CIP
                                                          AC

Visit us on the World Wide Web!
www.harperchildrens.com

One day a hungry robin saw an inchworm, green as an emerald, sitting on a twig. He was about to gobble him up.

"Don't eat me. I am an inchworm. I am useful.
I measure things."
"Is that so!" said the robin. "Then measure my tail!"

"That's easy," said the inchworm.
"One, two, three, four, five inches."

"Just think," said the robin, "my tail is five inches long!"
And with the inchworm, he flew to where other birds needed to be measured.

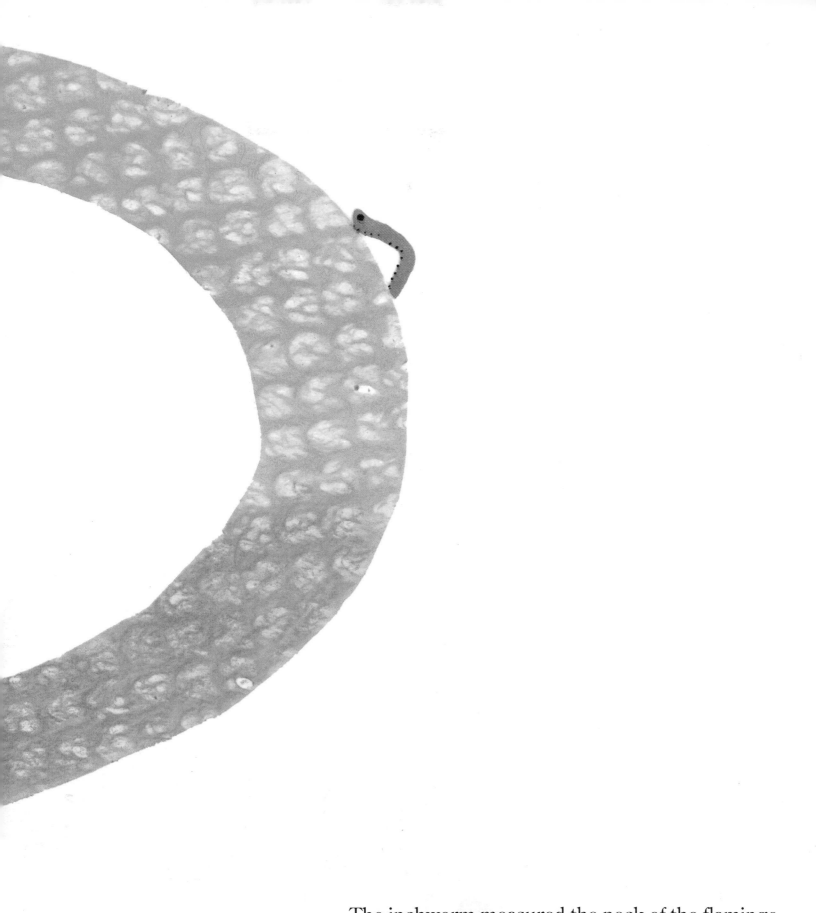

The inchworm measured the neck of the flamingo.

He measured the toucan's beak...

the legs of the heron...

the tail of the pheasant...

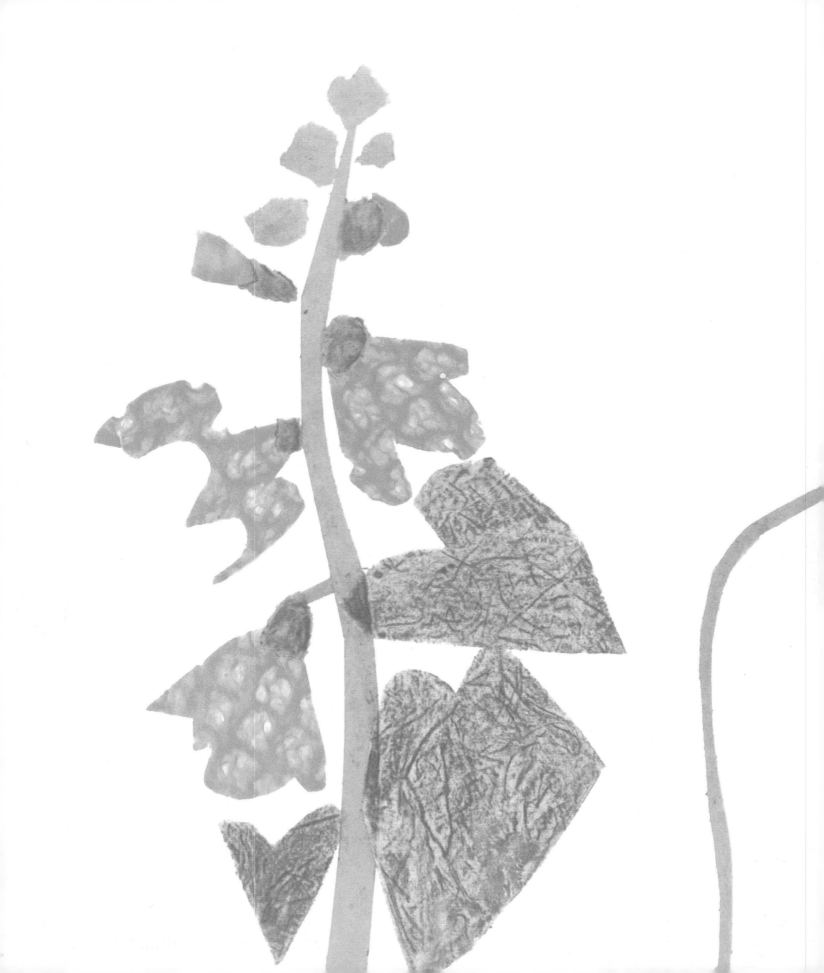

and the whole hummingbird.

One morning, the nightingale met the inchworm.

"Measure my song," said the nightingale.

"But how can I do that?" said the inchworm. "I measure things, not songs.

"Measure my song or I'll eat you for breakfast," said the nightingale.

Then the inchworm had an idea.

"I'll try," he said, "go ahead and sing."

The nightingale sang and the inchworm measured away.

He measured and measured...

Inch by Inch...

until he inched out of sight.

More Picture Books
by Leo Lionni

Little Blue and Little Yellow. Here is a fanciful story that captures the joy and pleasure of friendship between two children as it introduces certain basic concepts about color. (ISBN 0-688-13285-5)

On My Beach There Are Many Pebbles. Challenge young readers to look closely at the most ordinary of objects to discover the extraordinary beauty and majesty of each. (ISBN 0-688-13284-7)

Available wherever books are sold.